W9-ANT-087

AVENGERS K #6
ASSEMBLING THE AVENGERS

S.H.I.E.L.D. Agents Clint Barton, A.K.A. Hawkeye, and Phil Coulson have their hands full in New Mexico when the otherworldly Destroyer unleashes an assault against innocent bystanders. Only with Thor's help is the Destroyer finally disarmed and taken into S.H.I.E.L.D. custody. But S.H.I.E.L.D. Director Nick Fury's problems continue to mount as Gen. Thaddeus "Thunderbolt" Ross accesses the extra-governmental organization's database.

JIM ZUB
SCRIPT

WOO BIN CHOI WITH **JAE SUNG LEE**
ART

MIN JU LEE
INKS

JAE WOONG LEE, HEE YE CHO & IN YOUNG LEE
COLORS

VC's CORY PETIT
LETTERS

WOO BIN CHOI WITH **JAE SUNG LEE, MIN JU LEE, JAE WOONG LEE & HEE YE CHO**
COVER ART

Adapted from *MARVEL'S AVENGERS PRELUDE: FURY'S BIG WEEK #1-4*.
Adaptations written by SI YEON PARK and translated by JI EUN PARK

AVENGERS created by STAN LEE and JACK KIRBY

Original comics written by CHRIS YOST and ERIC PEARSON;
and illustrated by LUKE ROSS, DANIEL HOR, AGUSTIN PADILLA, DON HO,
WELLINTON ALVES, RICK KETCHAM, MARK PENNINGTON and CHRIS SOTOMAYOR

Editor SARAH BRUNSTAD
Manager, Licensed Publishing JEFF REINGOLD
VP Brand Management & Development, Asia C.B. CEBULSKI
VP Production & Special Projects JEFF YOUNGQUIST
SVP Print, Sales & Marketing DAVID GABRIEL
Associate Manager, Digital Assets JOE HOCHSTEIN
Associate Managing Editor KATERI WOODY
Assistant Editor CAITLIN O'CONNELL
Senior Editor, Special Projects JENNIFER GRÜNWALD
Editor, Special Projects MARK D. BEAZLEY
Book Designer: ADAM DEL RE

Editor In Chief AXEL ALONSO
Chief Creative Officer JOE QUESADA
President DAN BUCKLEY
Executive Producer ALAN FINE

MARVEL

ABDO
Spotlight

AVENGERS ACTIVE ROSTER

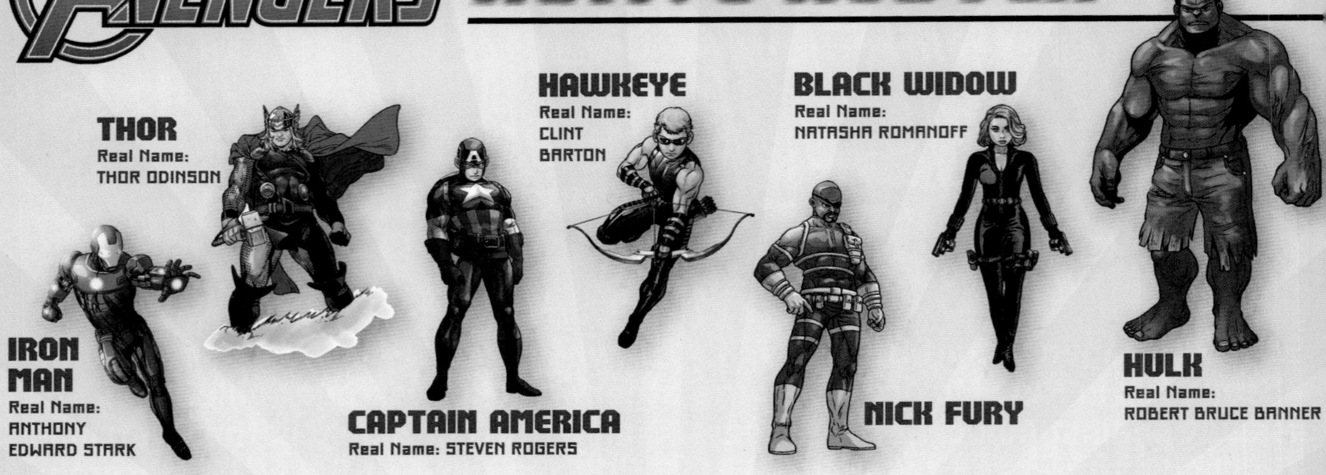
THOR
Real Name:
THOR ODINSON
HAWKEYE
Real Name:
CLINT
BARTON
BLACK WIDOW
Real Name:
NATASHA ROMANOFF
IRON
MAN
Real Name:
ANTHONY
EDWARD STARK
CAPTAIN AMERICA
Real Name: STEVEN ROGERS
NICK FURY
HULK
Real Name:
ROBERT BRUCE BANNER

EXTRAORDINARY ALLIES

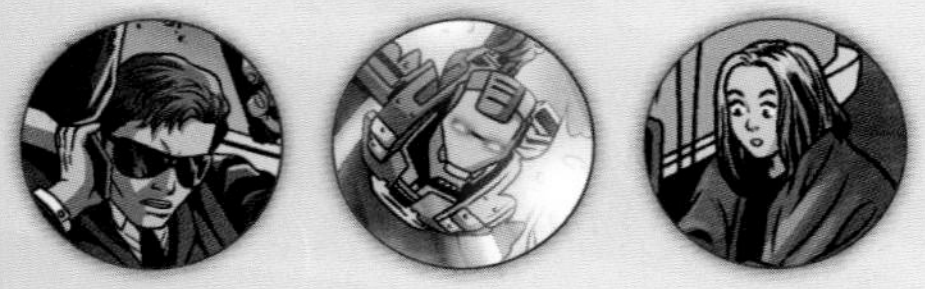

PHIL COULSON | WAR MACHINE | JANE FOSTER

AVENGERS MOST WANTED

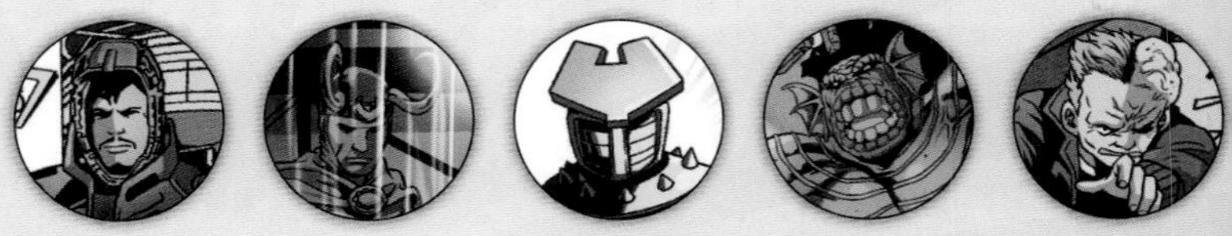

WHIPLASH | LOKI | DESTROYER | ABOMINATION | SAMUEL STERNS

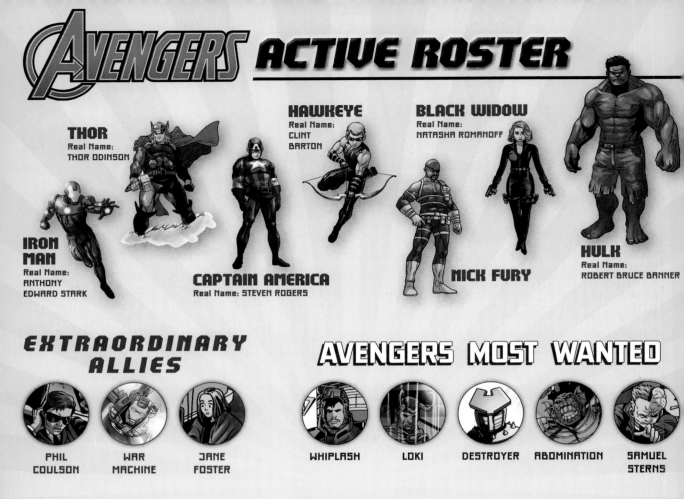

ABDOPUBLISHING.COM

Reinforced library bound edition published in 2018 by Spotlight, a division of ABDO, PO Box 398166, Minneapolis, Minnesota 55439.
Spotlight produces high-quality reinforced library bound editions for schools and libraries. Published by agreement with Marvel Characters, Inc.
Printed in the United States of America, North Mankato, Minnesota.
092017 012018

MARVEL
marvelkids.com

THIS BOOK CONTAINS RECYCLED MATERIALS

PUBLISHER'S CATALOGING-IN-PUBLICATION DATA

Names: Zub, Jim, author. | Choi, Woo Bin; Lee, Jae Sung; Lee, Min Ju; Lee, Jae Woong; Cho, Hee Ye; Lee, In Young, illustrators.
Title: Assembling the Avengers / writer: Jim Zub ; art: Woo Bin Choi; Jae Sung Lee; Min Ju Lee; Jae Woong Lee; Hee Ye Cho; In Young Lee.
Description: Minneapolis, MN : Spotlight, 2018 | Series: Avengers K Set 3
Summary: With a changing world full of threats bigger than he could imagine, S.H.I.E.L.D. director Nick Fury struggles to follow orders from the World Security Council. He calls upon Agent Coulson, Hawkeye, and Black Widow for aid to search for the missing Captain America, help Tony Stark fix his failing arc reactor in his chest, stop the Hulk from going on a rampage, and unearth an alien object, followed shortly by its electrifying owner.
Identifiers: LCCN 2017941923 | ISBN 9781532141478 (v.1 ; lib. bdg.) | ISBN 9781532141485 (v.2 ; lib. bdg.) | ISBN 9781532141492 (v.3 ; lib. bdg.) | ISBN 9781532141508 (v.4 ; lib. bdg.) | ISBN 9781532141515 (v.5 ; lib. bdg.) | ISBN 9781532141522 (v.6 ; lib. bdg.) | ISBN 9781532141539 (v.7 ; lib.bdg.)
Subjects: LCSH: Avengers (ficitious character)--Juvenile fiction. | Super heroes--Juvenile fiction. | Graphic Novels--Juvenile fiction. | Media Tie-in--Juvenile fiction.
Classification: DDC 741.5--dc23
LC record available at http://lccn.loc.gov/2017941923

ABDO
Spotlight

A Division of ABDO
abdopublishing.com

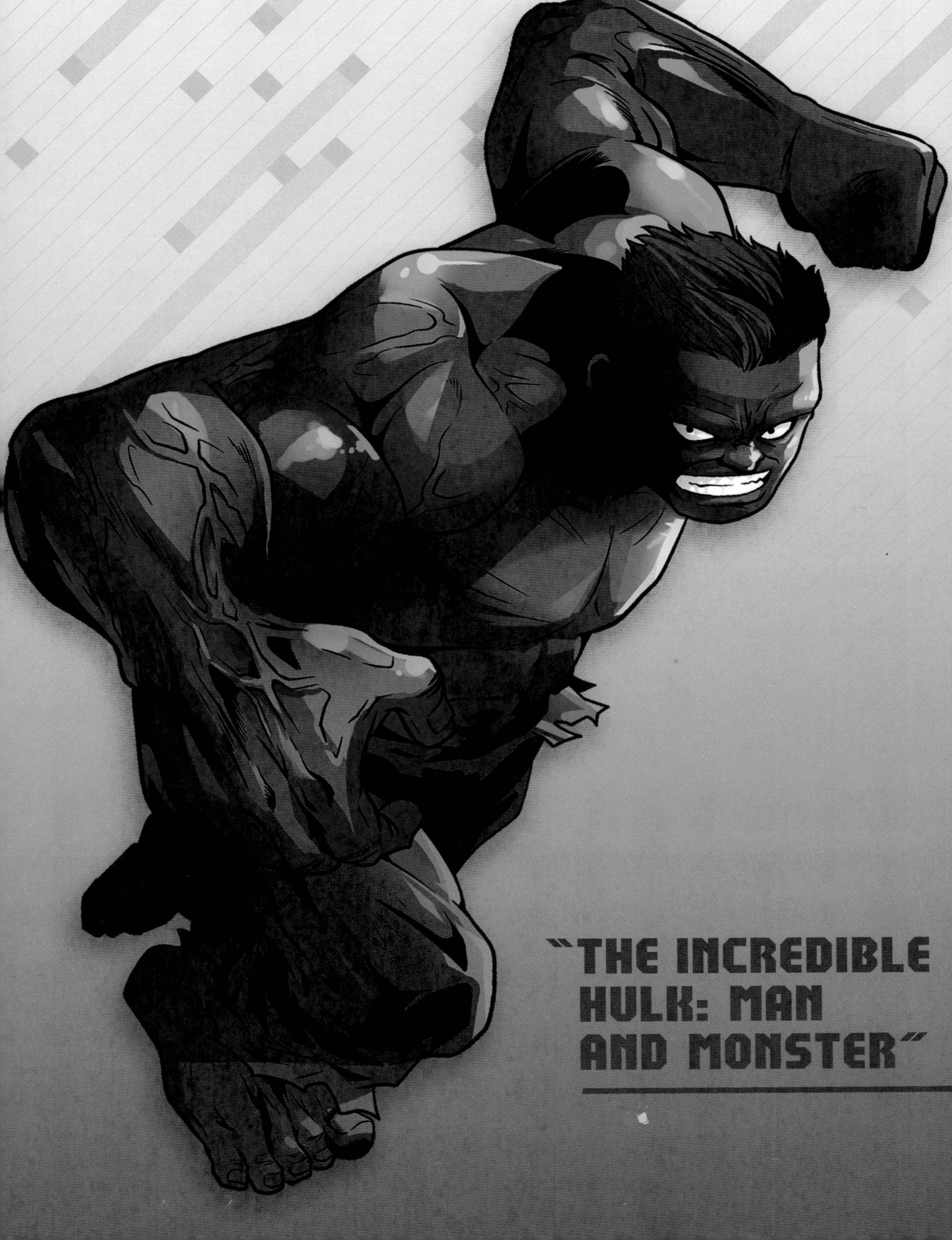

"THE INCREDIBLE HULK: MAN AND MONSTER"

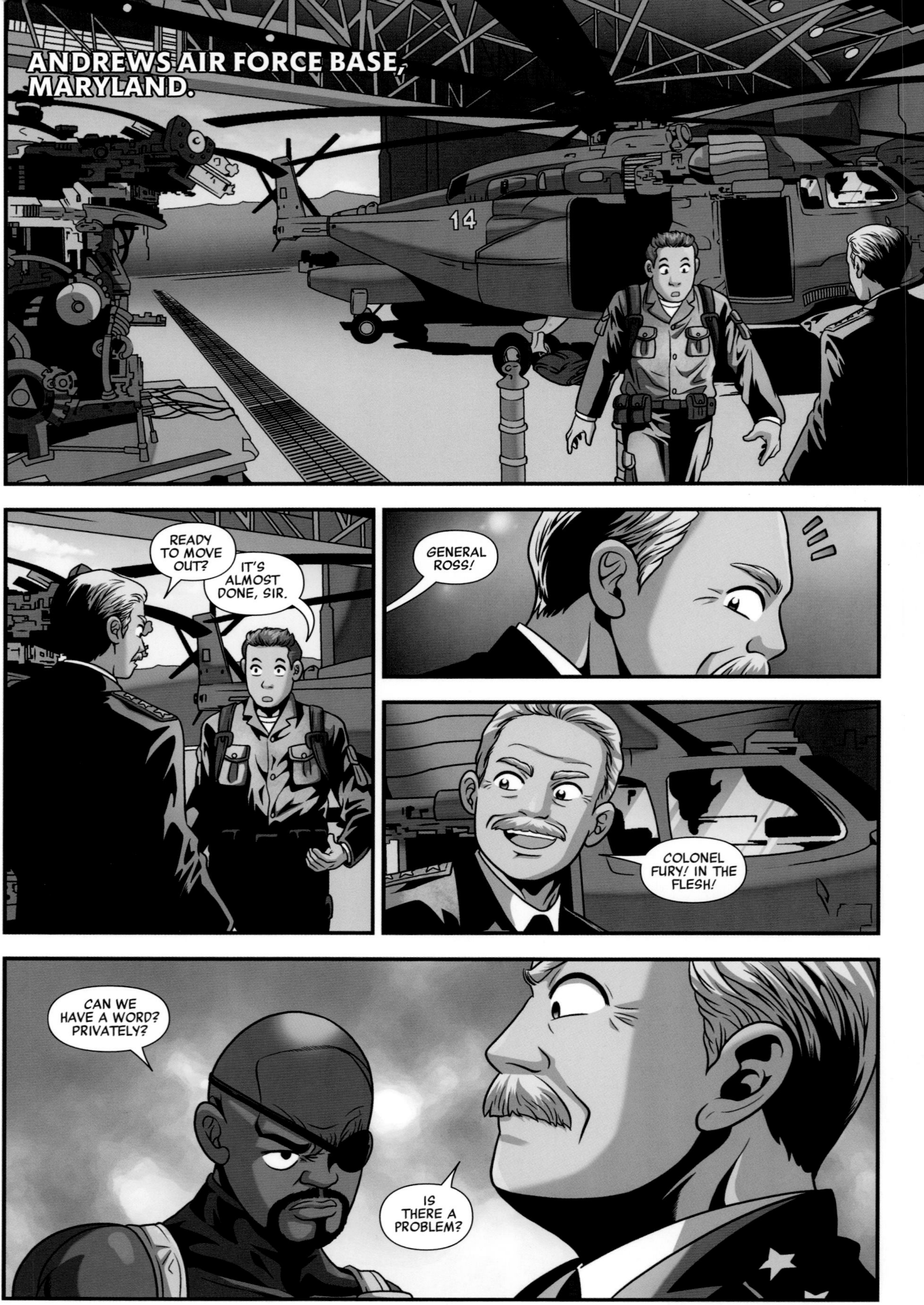
ANDREWS AIR FORCE BASE, MARYLAND.
READY TO MOVE OUT?
IT'S ALMOST DONE, SIR.
GENERAL ROSS!
COLONEL FURY! IN THE FLESH!
CAN WE HAVE A WORD? PRIVATELY?
IS THERE A PROBLEM?

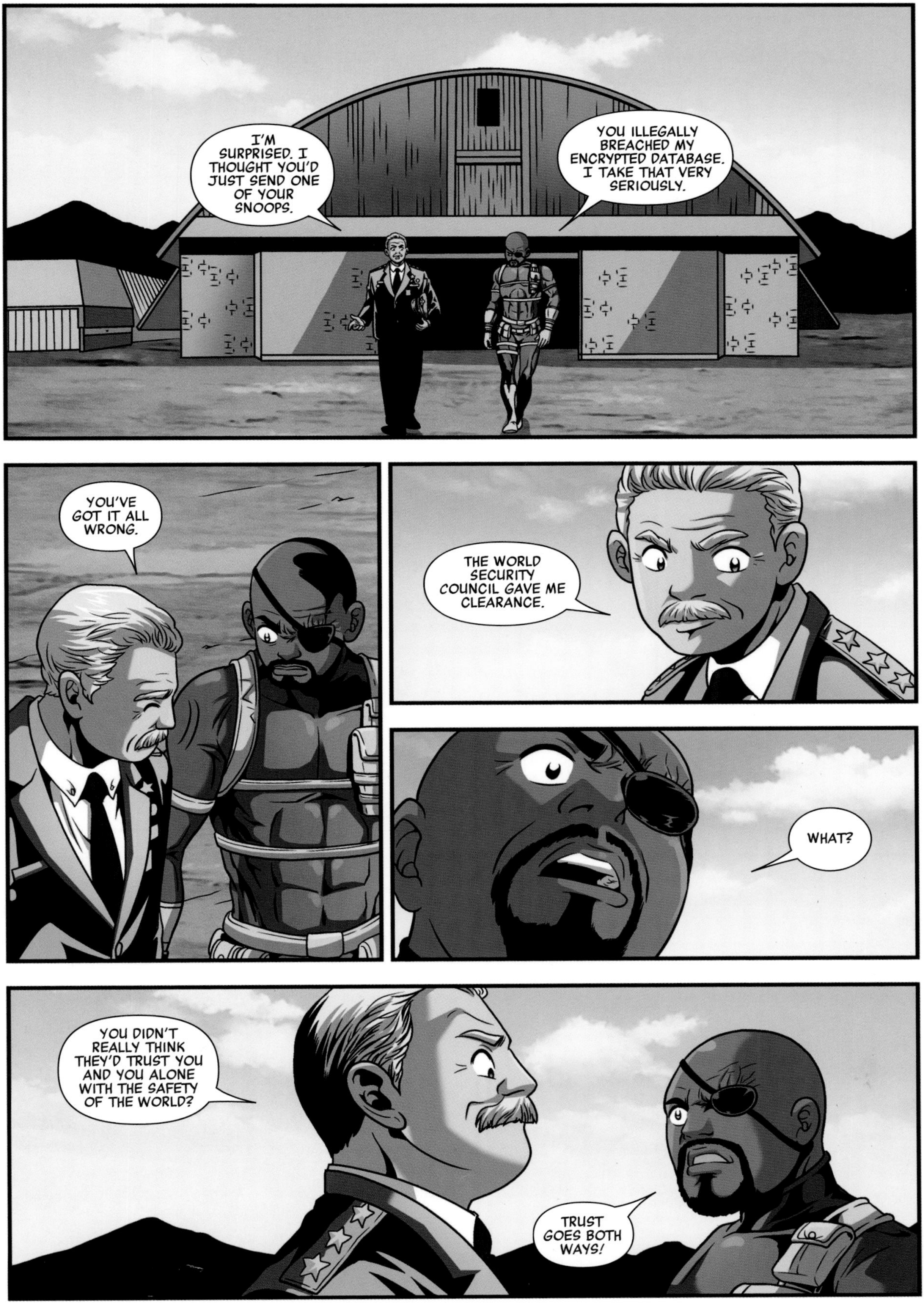
I'M SURPRISED. I THOUGHT YOU'D JUST SEND ONE OF YOUR SNOOPS.
YOU ILLEGALLY BREACHED MY ENCRYPTED DATABASE. I TAKE THAT VERY SERIOUSLY.
YOU'VE GOT IT ALL WRONG.
THE WORLD SECURITY COUNCIL GAVE ME CLEARANCE.
WHAT?
YOU DIDN'T REALLY THINK THEY'D TRUST YOU AND YOU ALONE WITH THE SAFETY OF THE WORLD?
TRUST GOES BOTH WAYS!

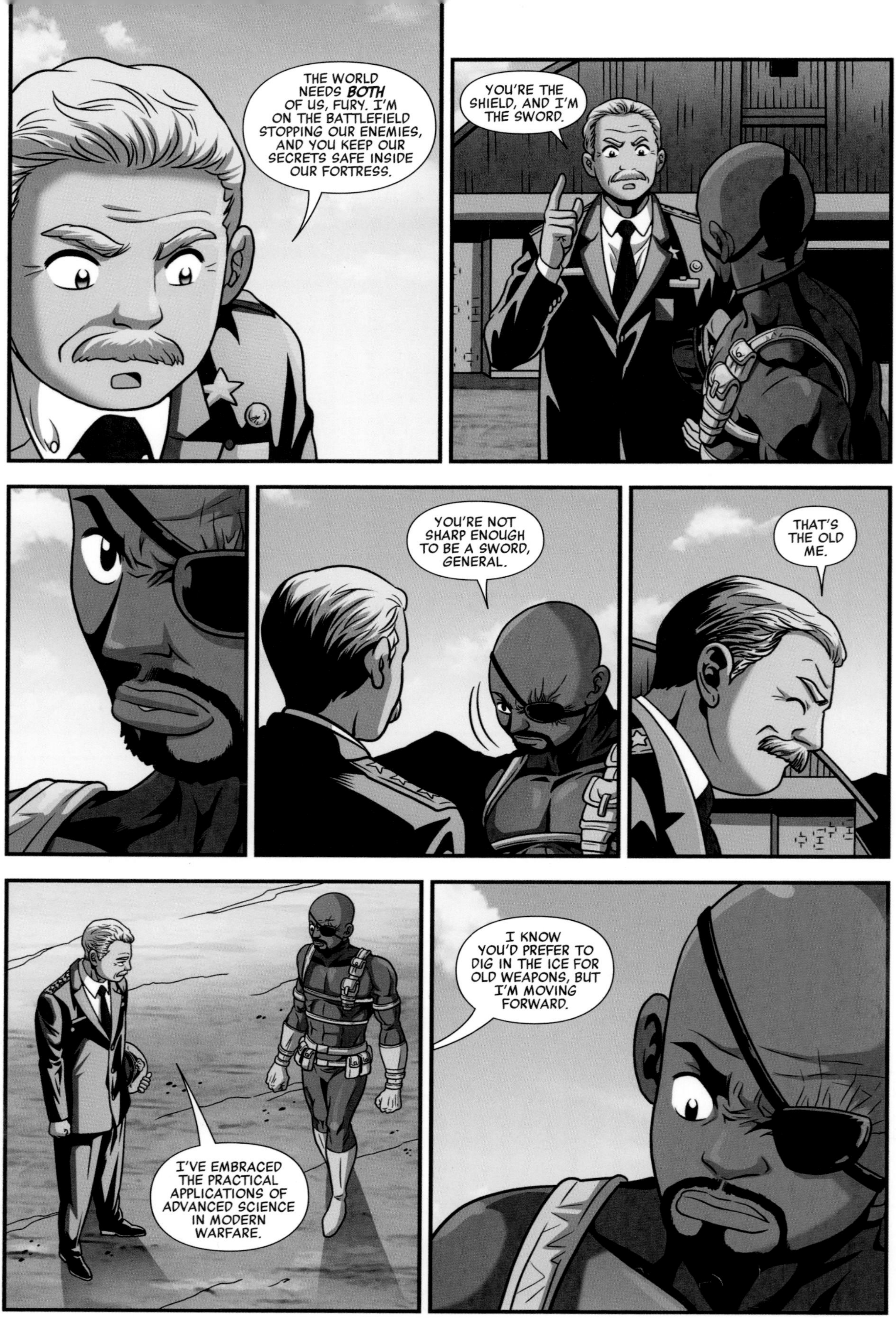
THE WORLD NEEDS BOTH OF US, FURY. I'M ON THE BATTLEFIELD STOPPING OUR ENEMIES, AND YOU KEEP OUR SECRETS SAFE INSIDE OUR FORTRESS.
YOU'RE THE SHIELD, AND I'M THE SWORD.
YOU'RE NOT SHARP ENOUGH TO BE A SWORD, GENERAL.
THAT'S THE OLD ME.
I'VE EMBRACED THE PRACTICAL APPLICATIONS OF ADVANCED SCIENCE IN MODERN WARFARE.
I KNOW YOU'D PREFER TO DIG IN THE ICE FOR OLD WEAPONS, BUT I'M MOVING FORWARD.

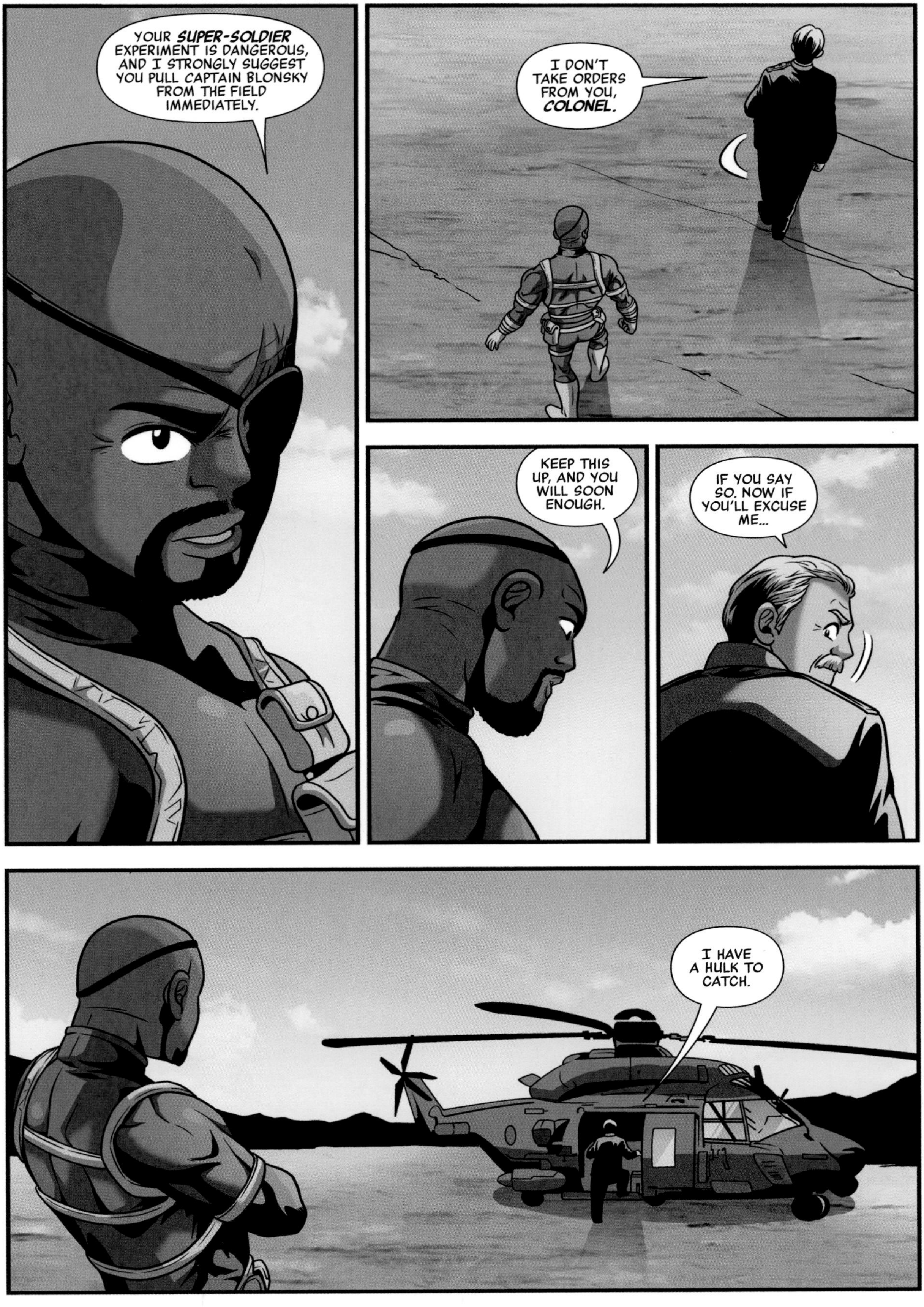
YOUR SUPER-SOLDIER EXPERIMENT IS DANGEROUS, AND I STRONGLY SUGGEST YOU PULL CAPTAIN BLONSKY FROM THE FIELD IMMEDIATELY.
I DON'T TAKE ORDERS FROM YOU, COLONEL.
KEEP THIS UP, AND YOU WILL SOON ENOUGH.
IF YOU SAY SO. NOW IF YOU'LL EXCUSE ME...
I HAVE A HULK TO CATCH.

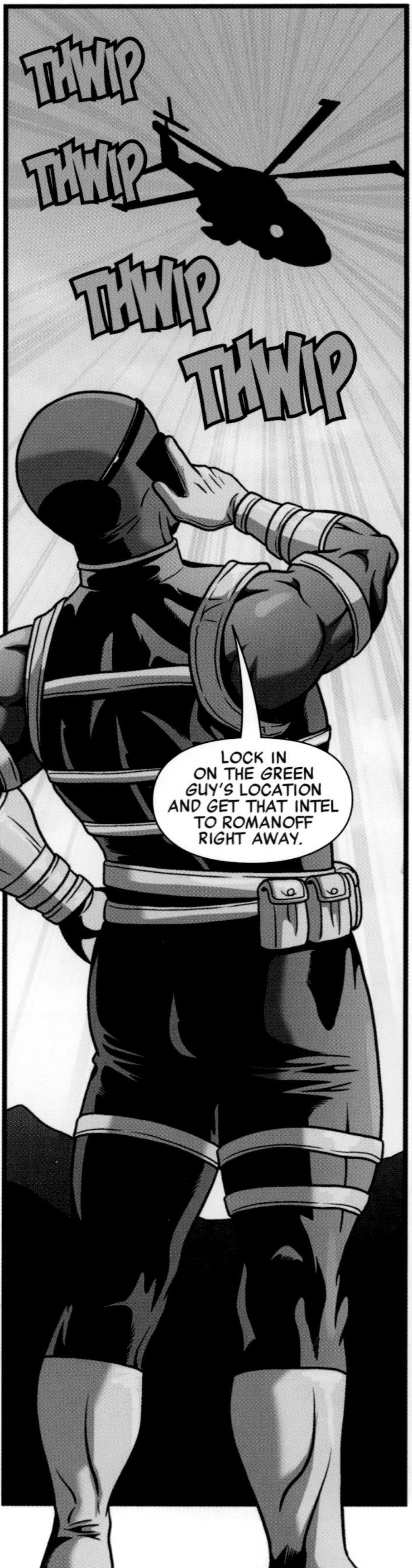
THWIP
THWIP
THWIP
THWIP
LOCK IN ON THE GREEN GUY'S LOCATION AND GET THAT INTEL TO ROMANOFF RIGHT AWAY.

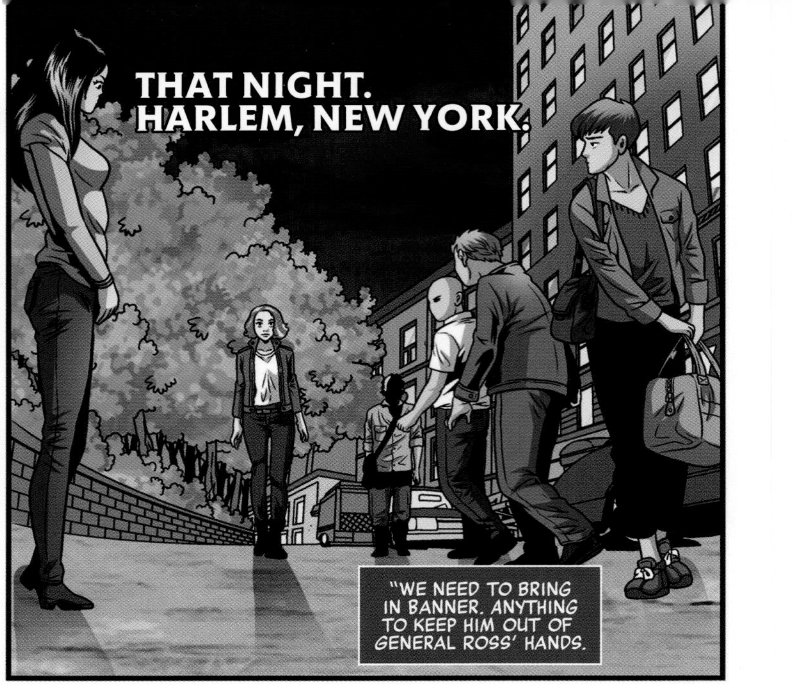
THAT NIGHT. HARLEM, NEW YORK.
"WE NEED TO BRING IN BANNER. ANYTHING TO KEEP HIM OUT OF GENERAL ROSS' HANDS.

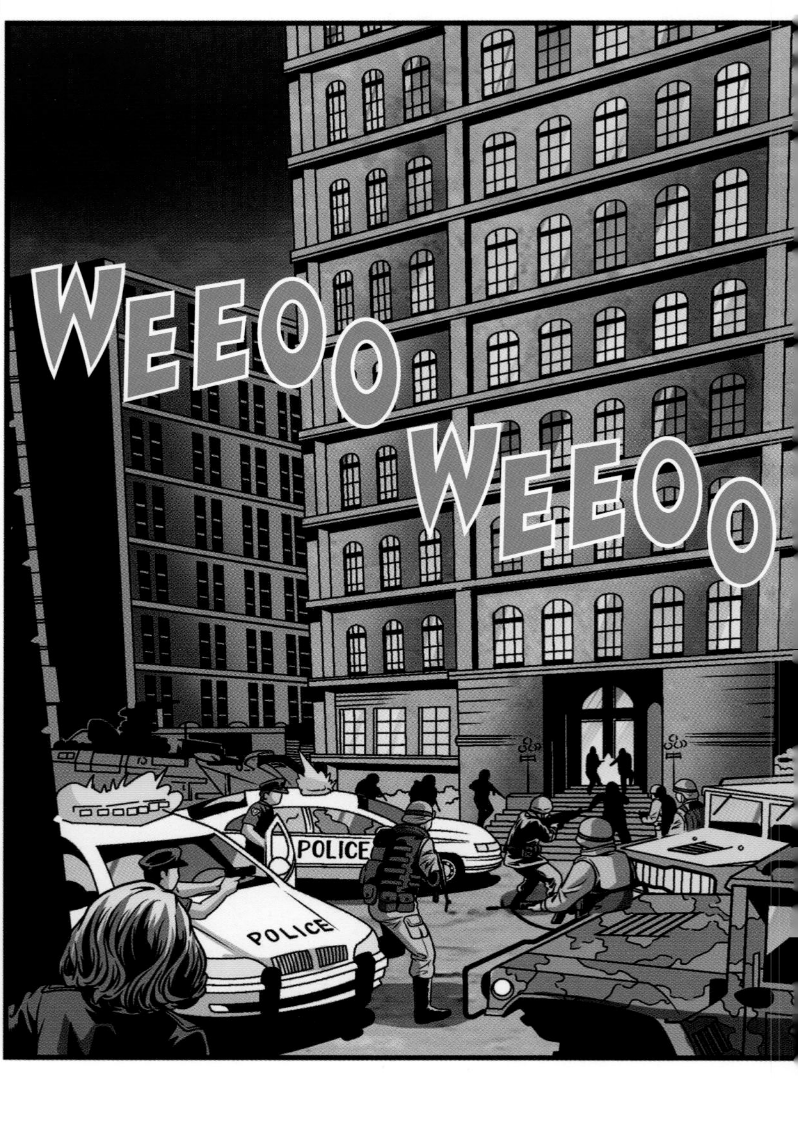
WEEOO
WEEOO
POLICE
POLICE

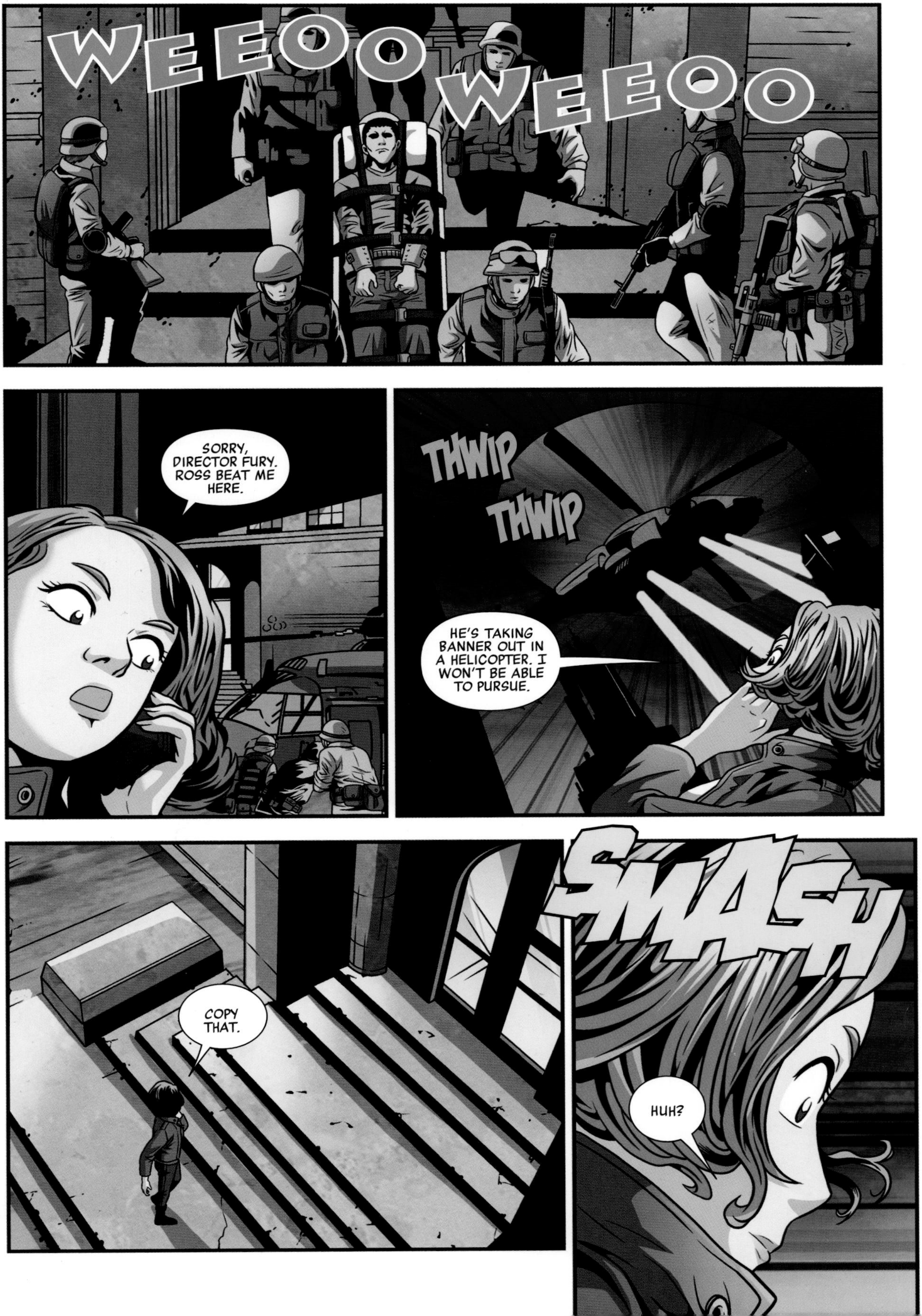
WEEOO WEEOO
SORRY, DIRECTOR FURY. ROSS BEAT ME HERE.
THWIP
THWIP
HE'S TAKING BANNER OUT IN A HELICOPTER. I WON'T BE ABLE TO PURSUE.
COPY THAT.
SMASH
HUH?

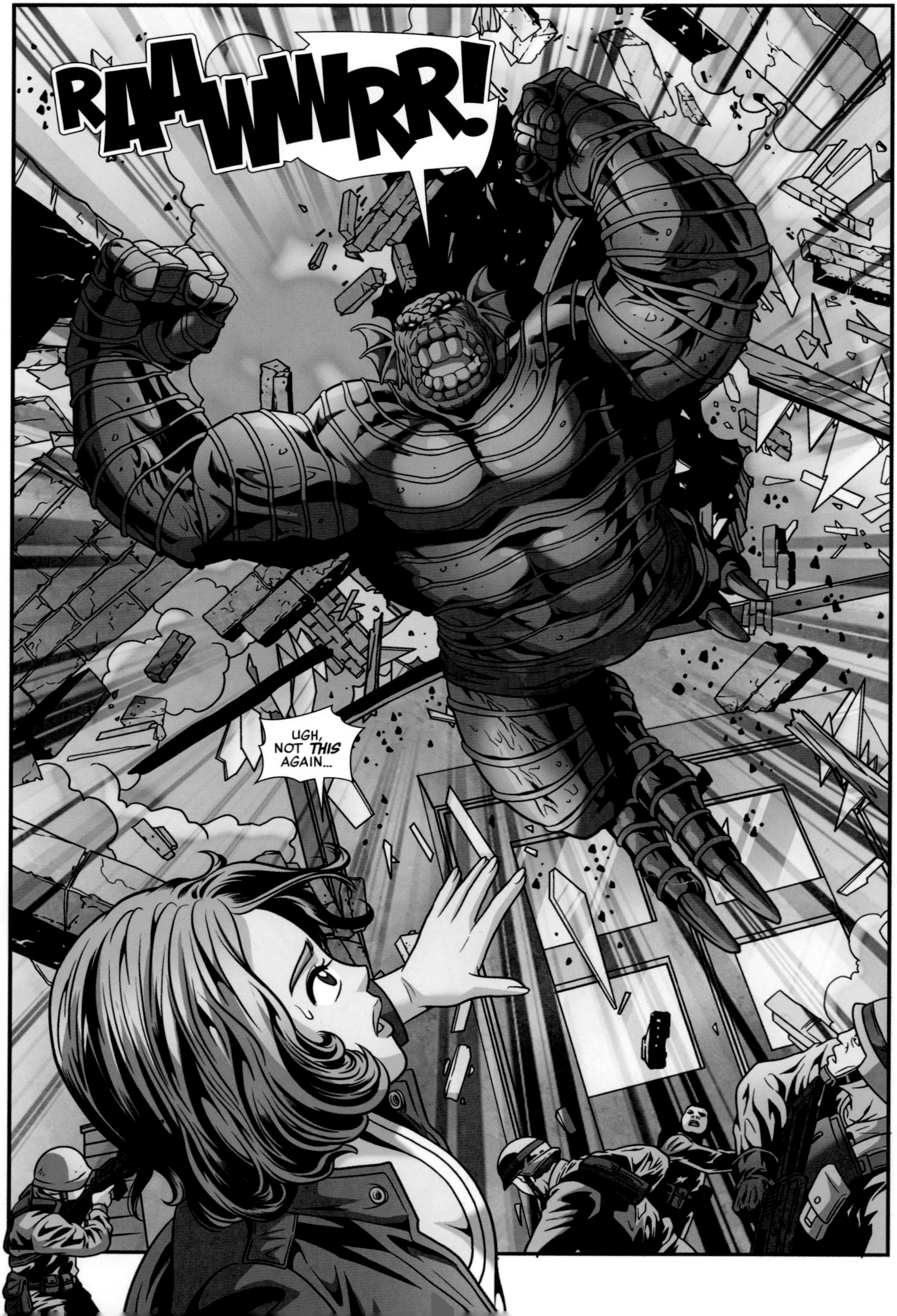
RAAWWRR!
UGH, NOT THIS AGAIN...

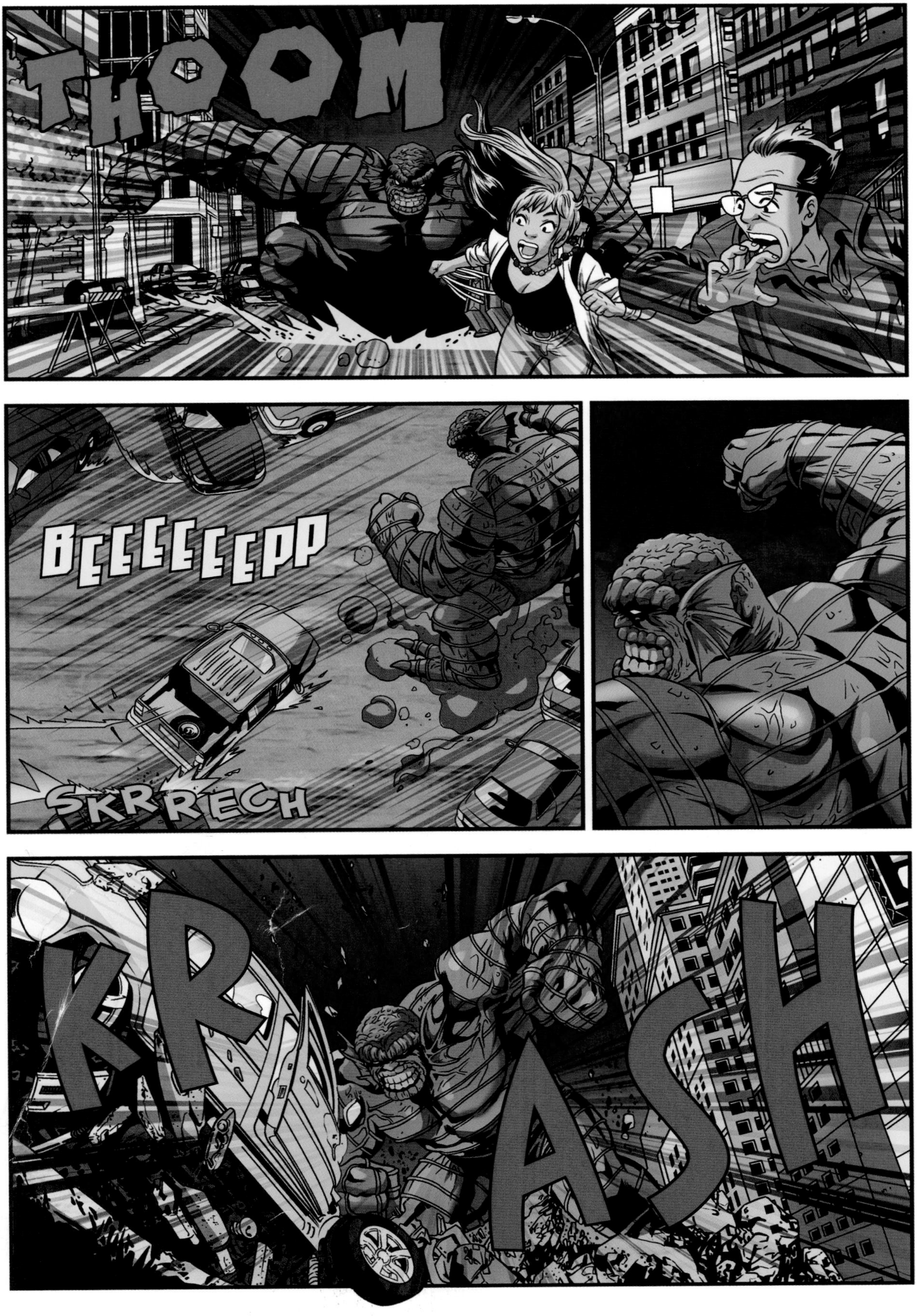
THOOM
BEEEEEEPP
SKRRECH
KRASH

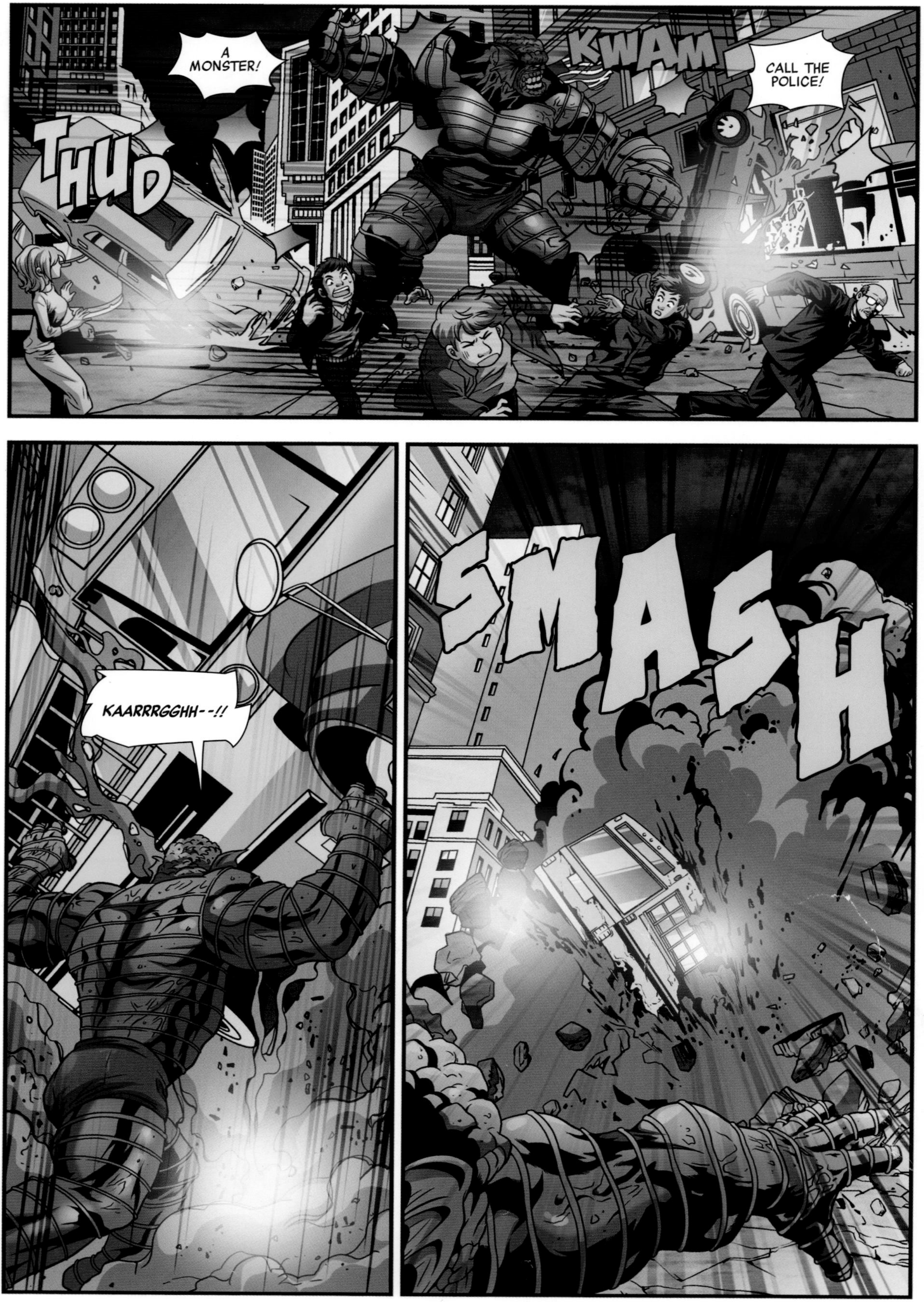
THUD
A MONSTER!
KWAM
CALL THE POLICE!
KAARRRGGHH--!!
SMASH

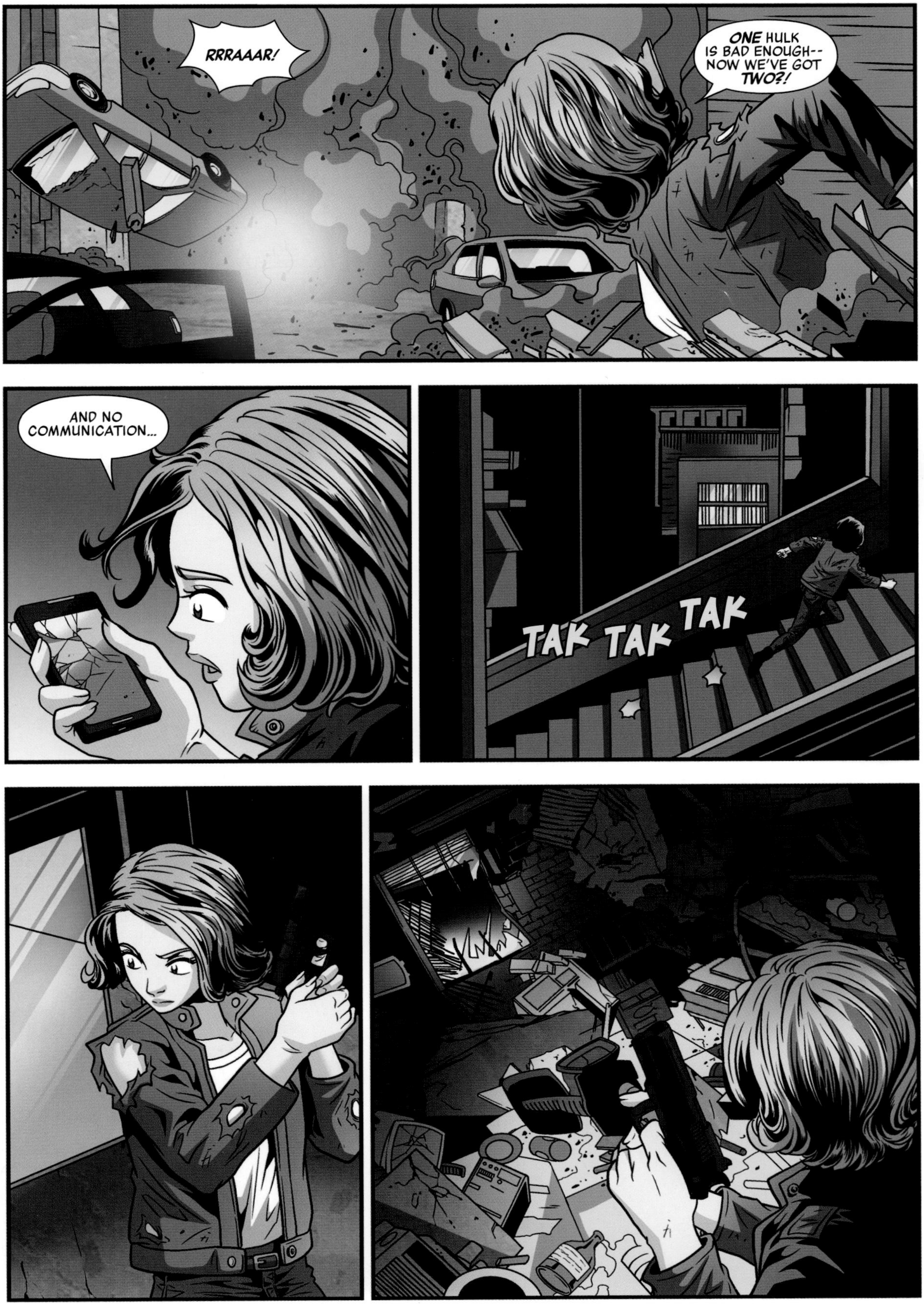
RRRAAAR!
ONE HULK IS BAD ENOUGH-- NOW WE'VE GOT TWO?!
AND NO COMMUNICATION...
TAK TAK TAK

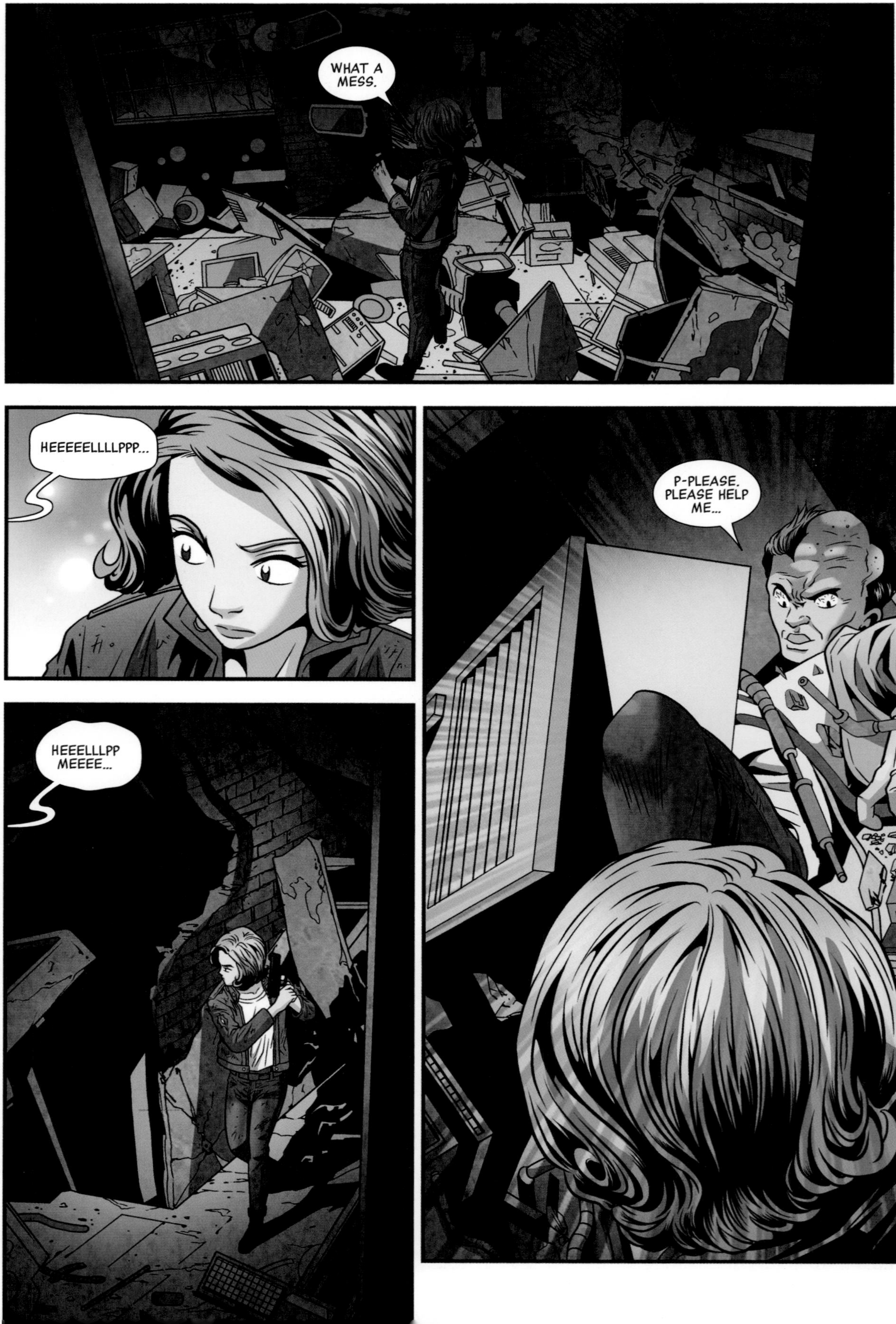
WHAT A MESS.
HEEEEELLLLPPP...
HEEELLLPP MEEEE...
P-PLEASE. PLEASE HELP ME...

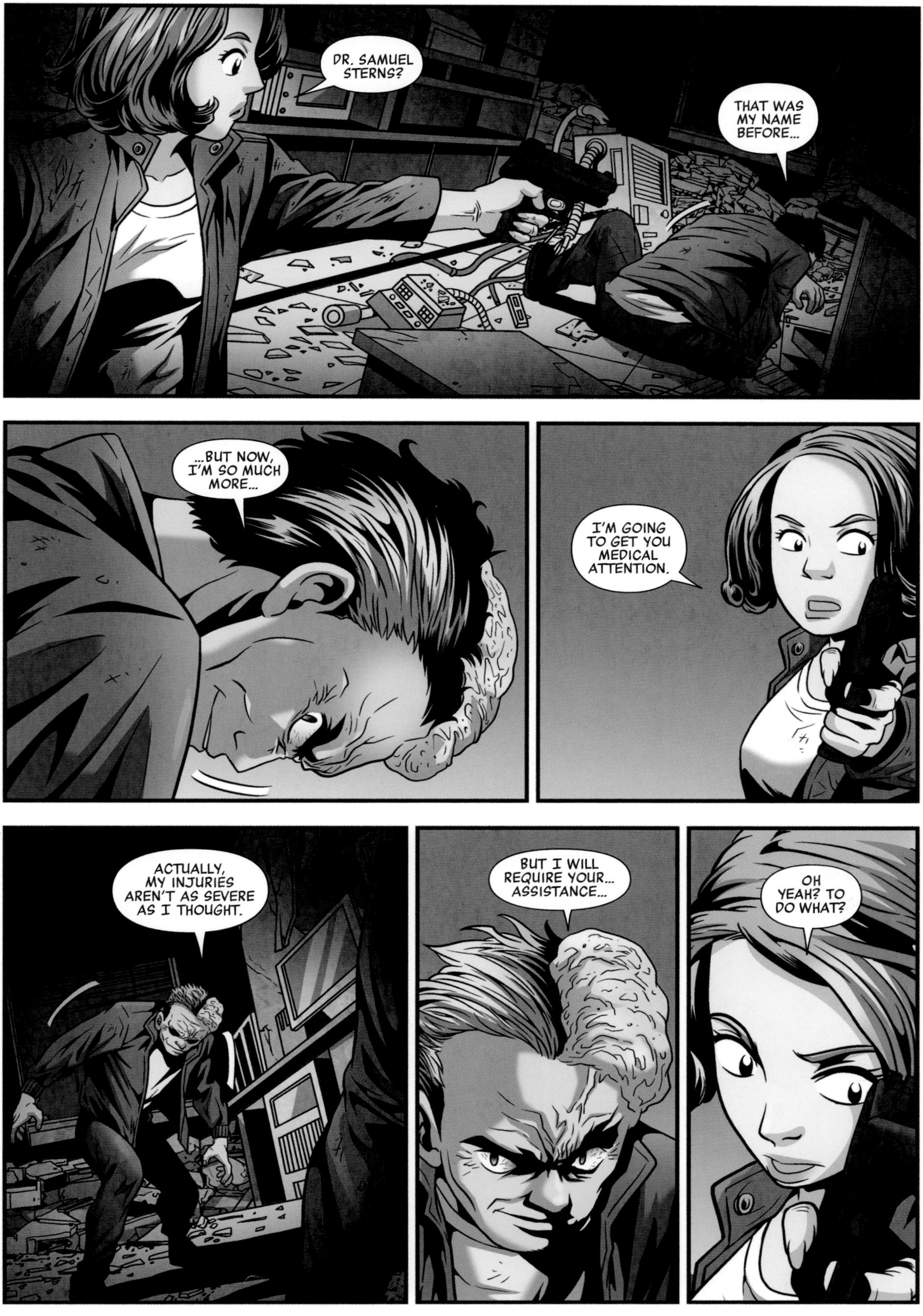
DR. SAMUEL STERNS?
THAT WAS MY NAME BEFORE...
...BUT NOW, I'M SO MUCH MORE...
I'M GOING TO GET YOU MEDICAL ATTENTION.
ACTUALLY, MY INJURIES AREN'T AS SEVERE AS I THOUGHT.
BUT I WILL REQUIRE YOUR... ASSISTANCE...
OH YEAH? TO DO WHAT?

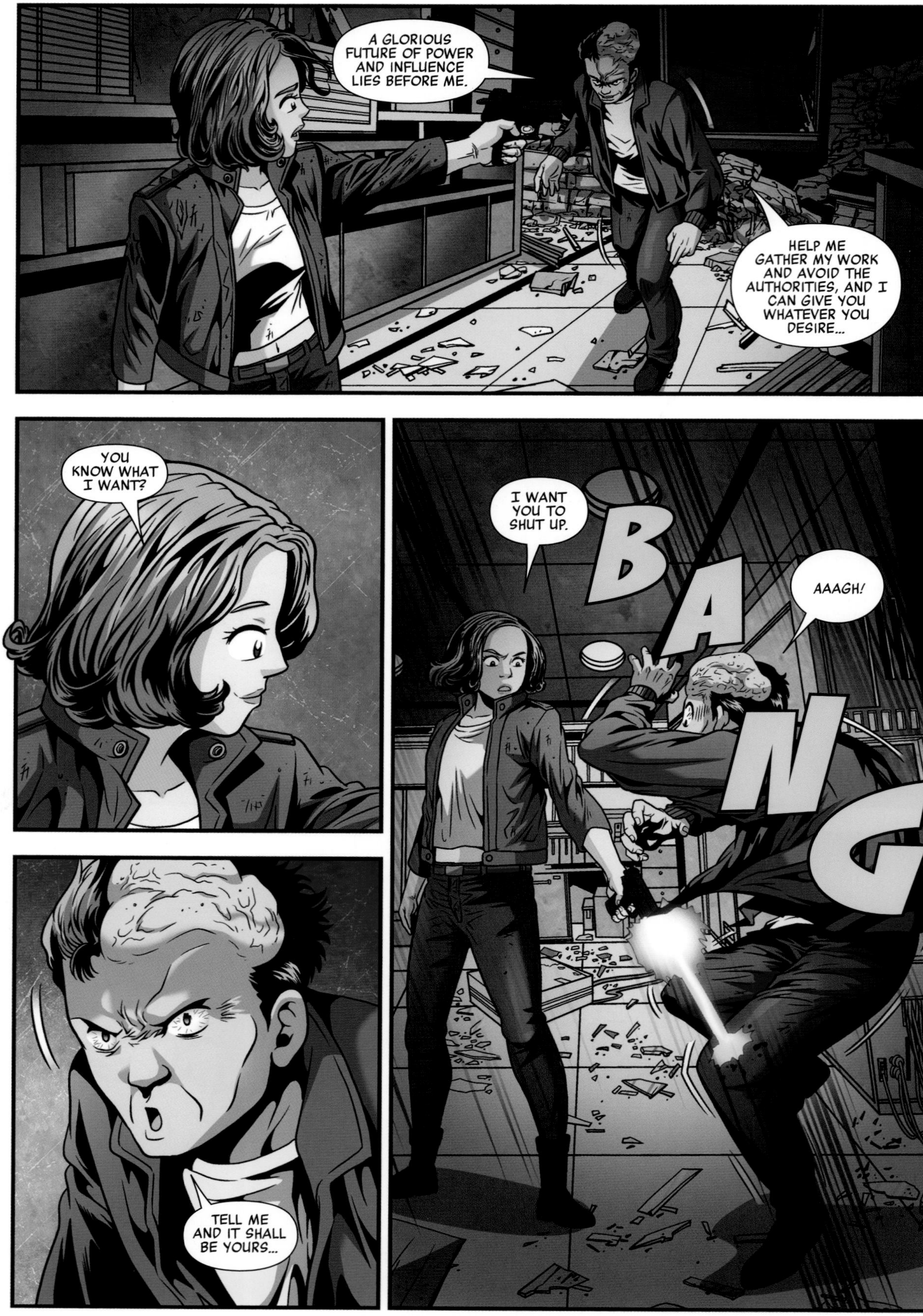
A GLORIOUS FUTURE OF POWER AND INFLUENCE LIES BEFORE ME.
HELP ME GATHER MY WORK AND AVOID THE AUTHORITIES, AND I CAN GIVE YOU WHATEVER YOU DESIRE...
YOU KNOW WHAT I WANT?
TELL ME AND IT SHALL BE YOURS...
I WANT YOU TO SHUT UP.
BANG
AAAGH!

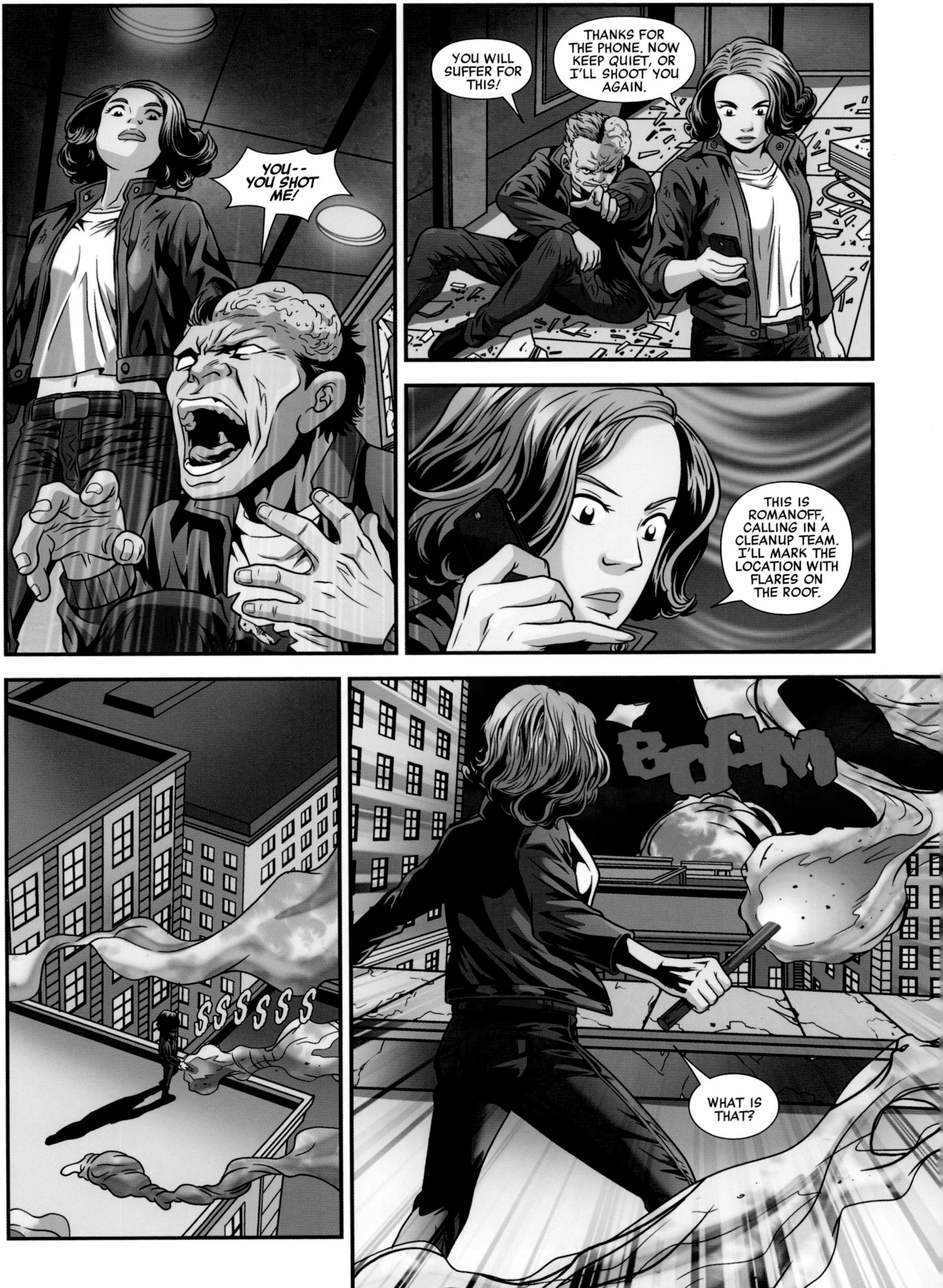
YOU--
YOU SHOT
ME!
YOU WILL
SUFFER FOR
THIS!
THANKS FOR
THE PHONE. NOW
KEEP QUIET, OR
I'LL SHOOT YOU
AGAIN.
THIS IS
ROMANOFF,
CALLING IN A
CLEANUP TEAM.
I'LL MARK THE
LOCATION WITH
FLARES ON
THE ROOF.
SSSSSS
BOOM
WHAT IS
THAT?

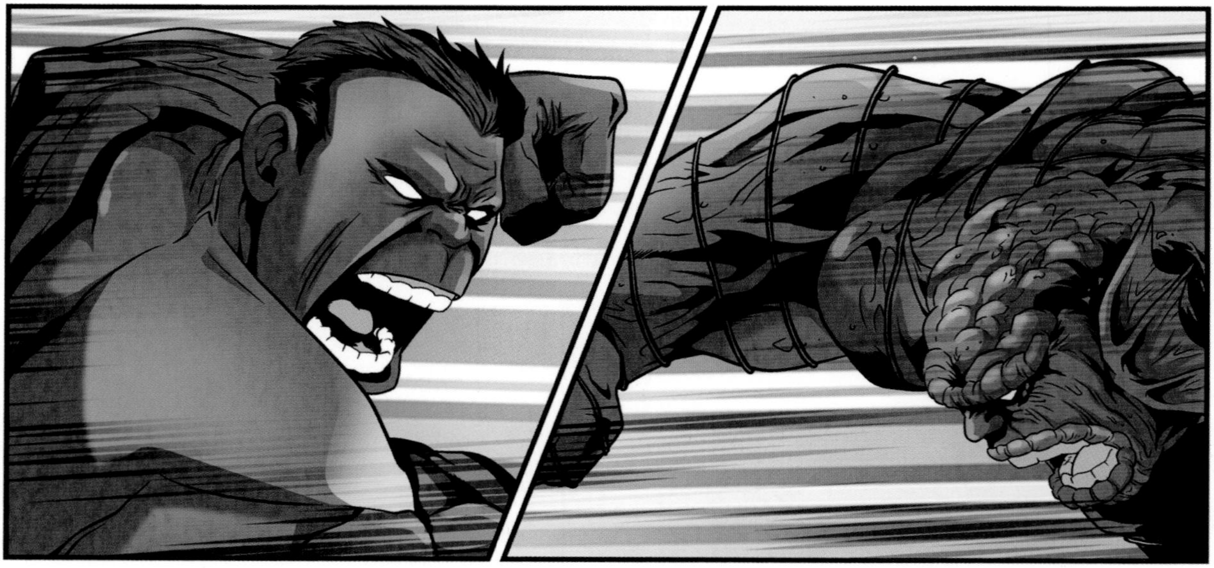

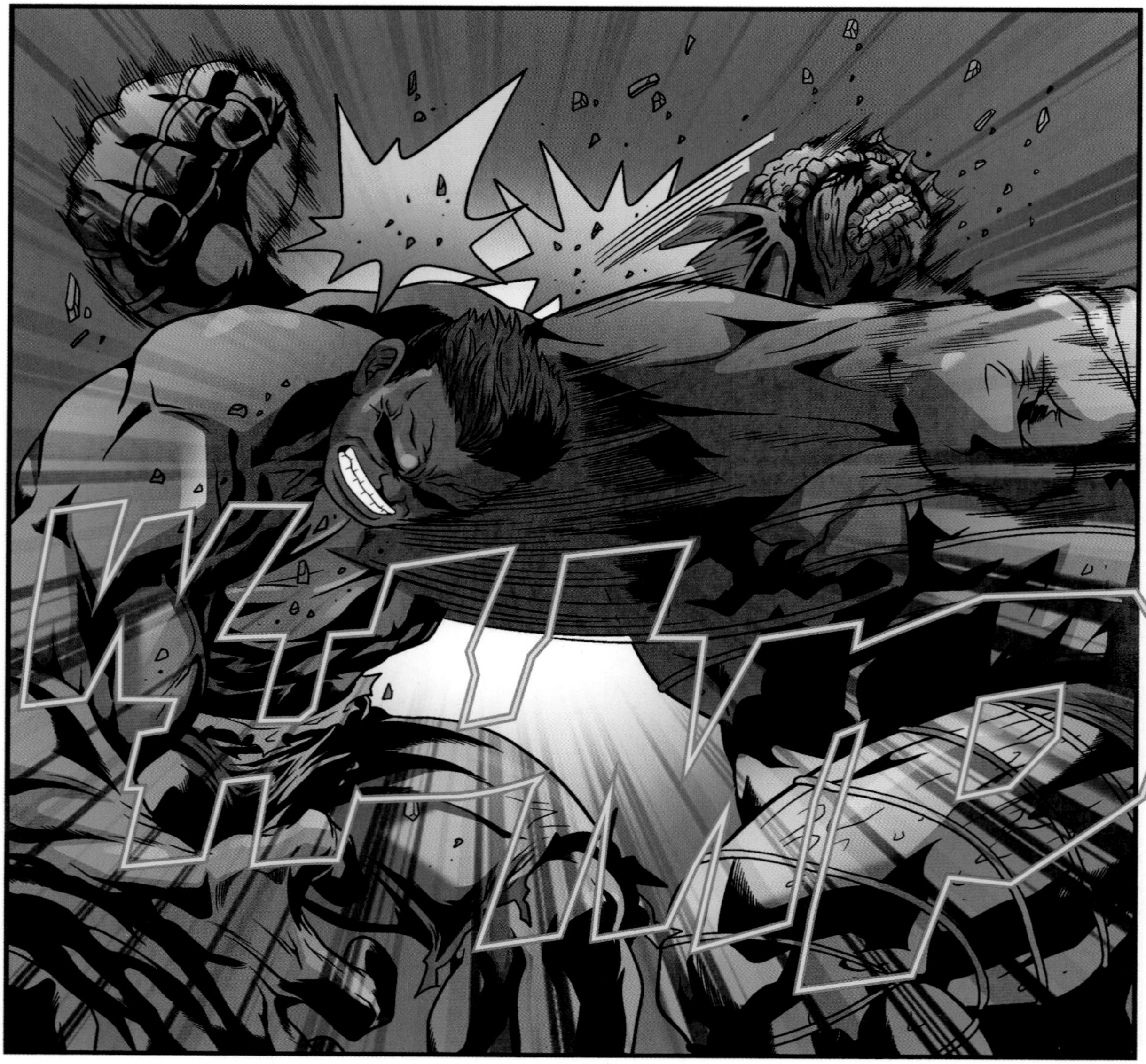

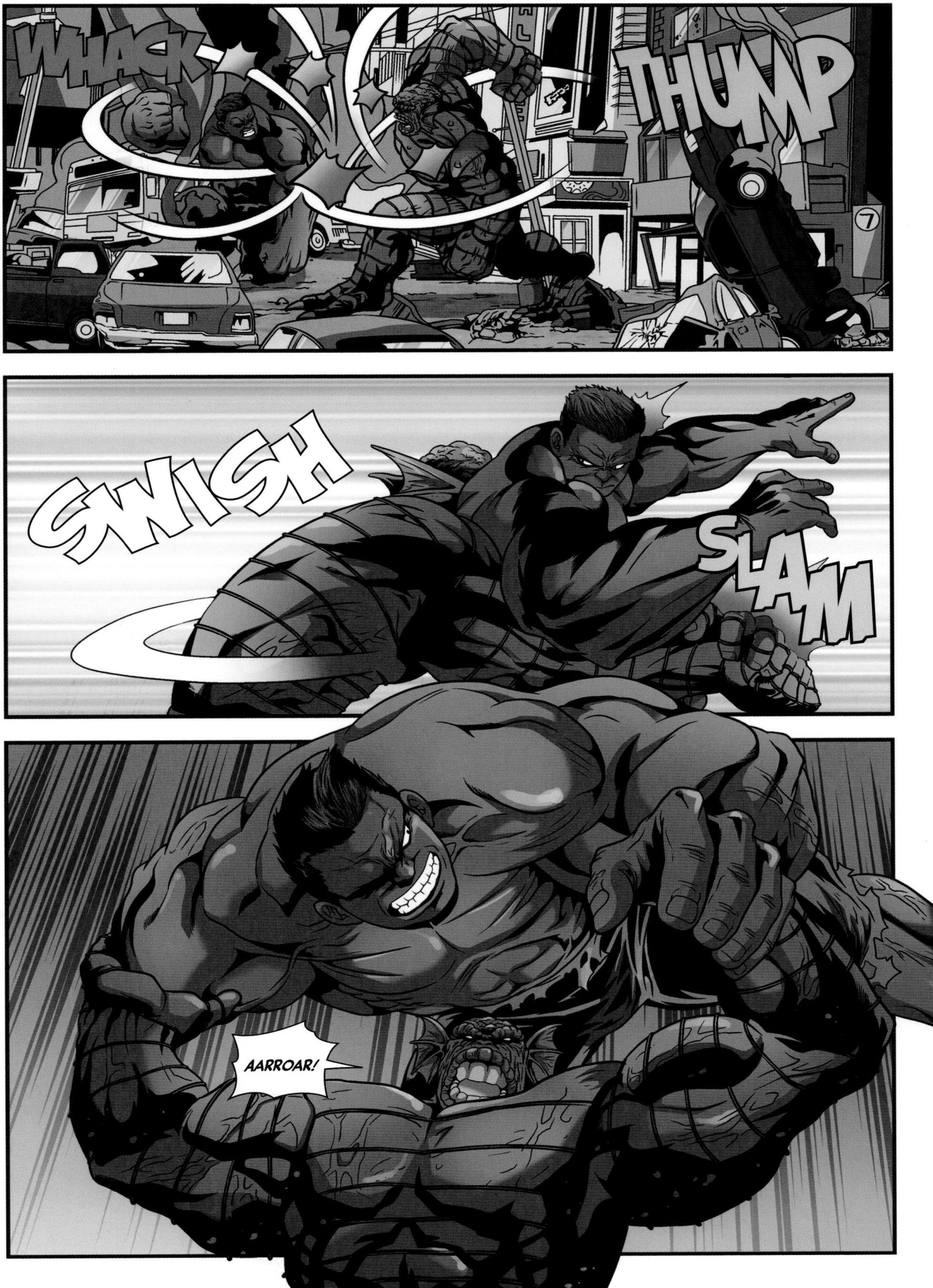
WHACK
THUMP
SWISH
SLAM
AARROAR!

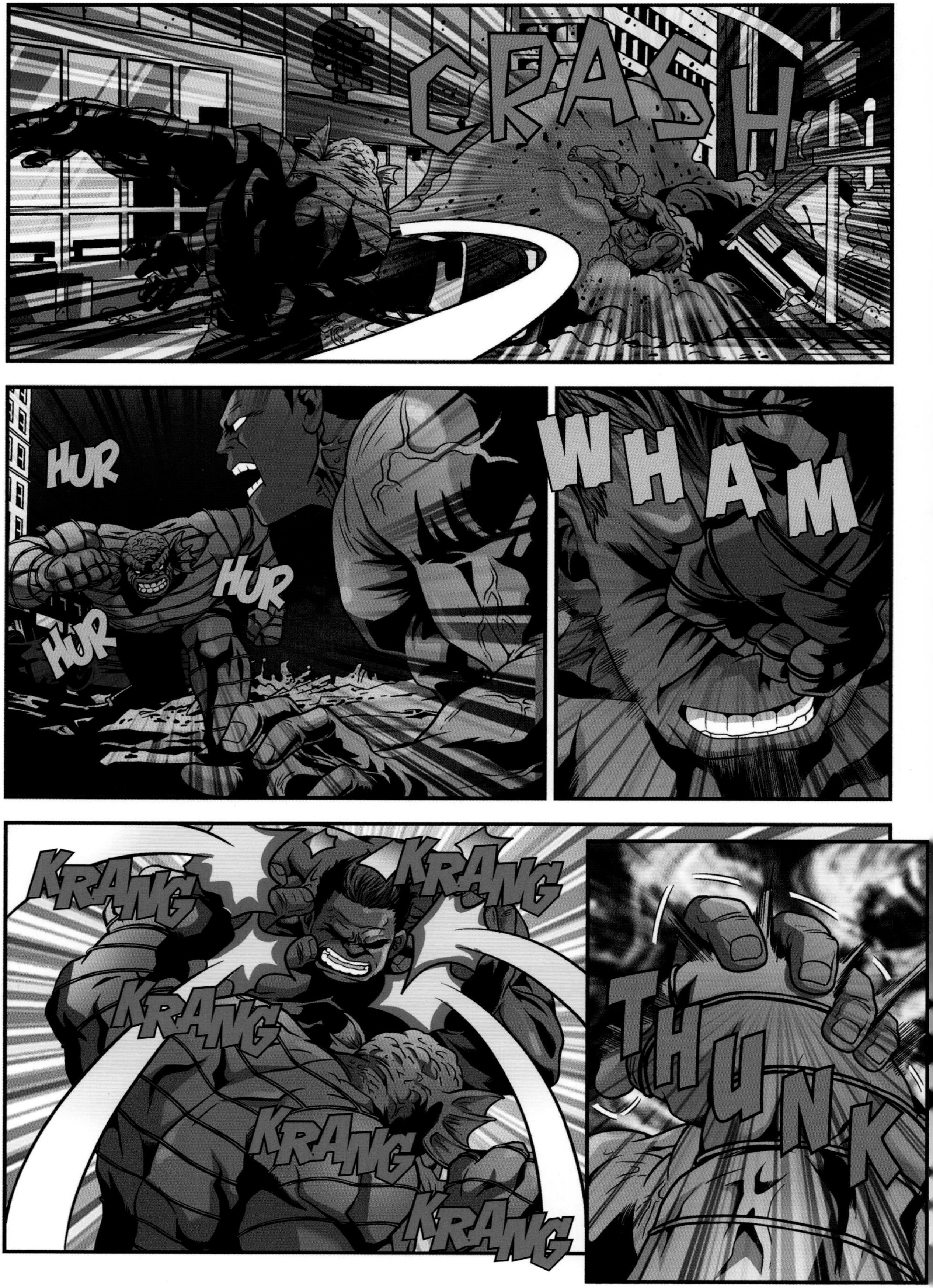
CRASH
HUR
HUR
HUR
WHAM
KRANG
KRANG
KRANG
KRANG
KRANG
THUNK

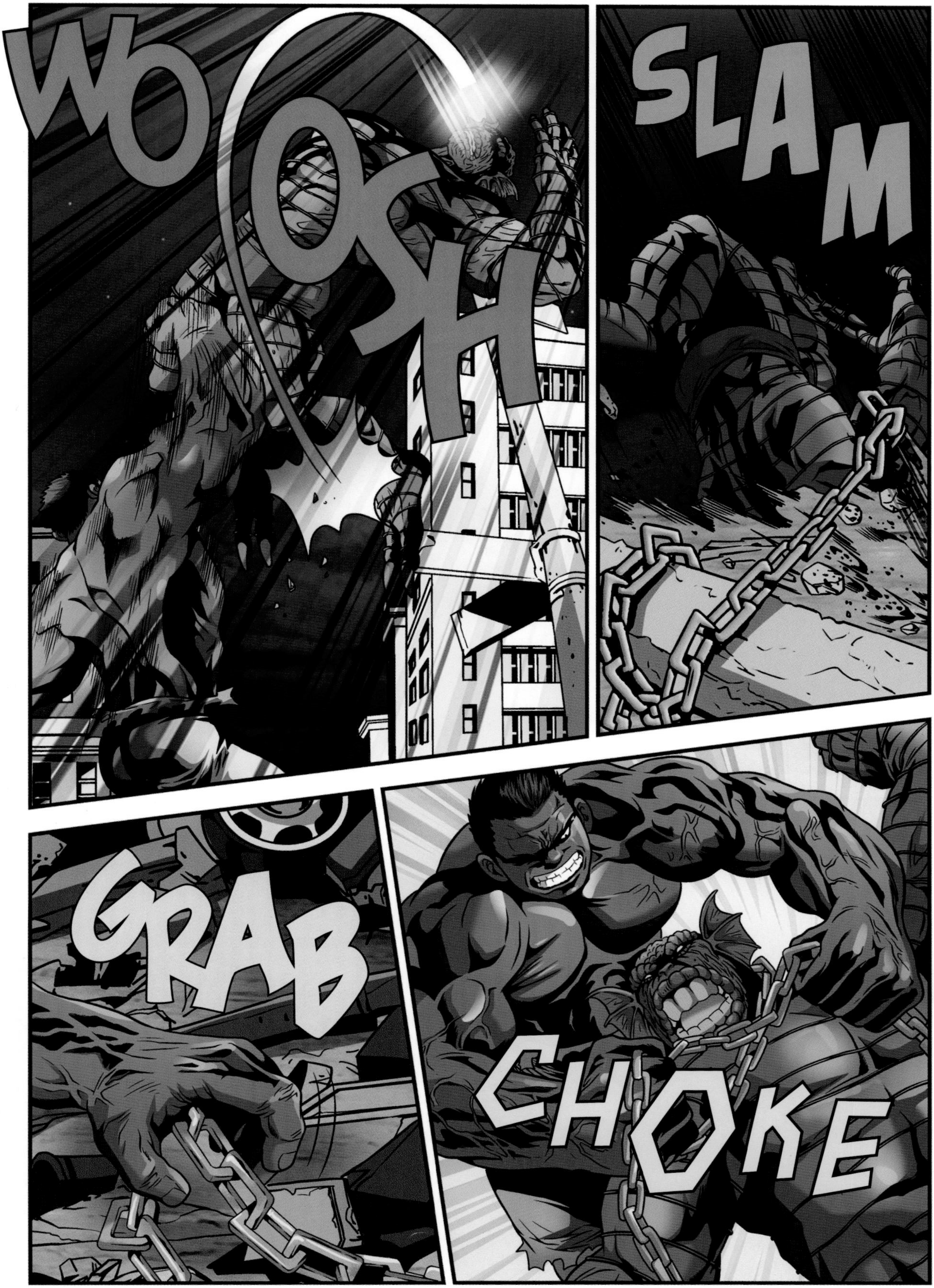
WOOSH
SLAM
GRAB
CHOKE

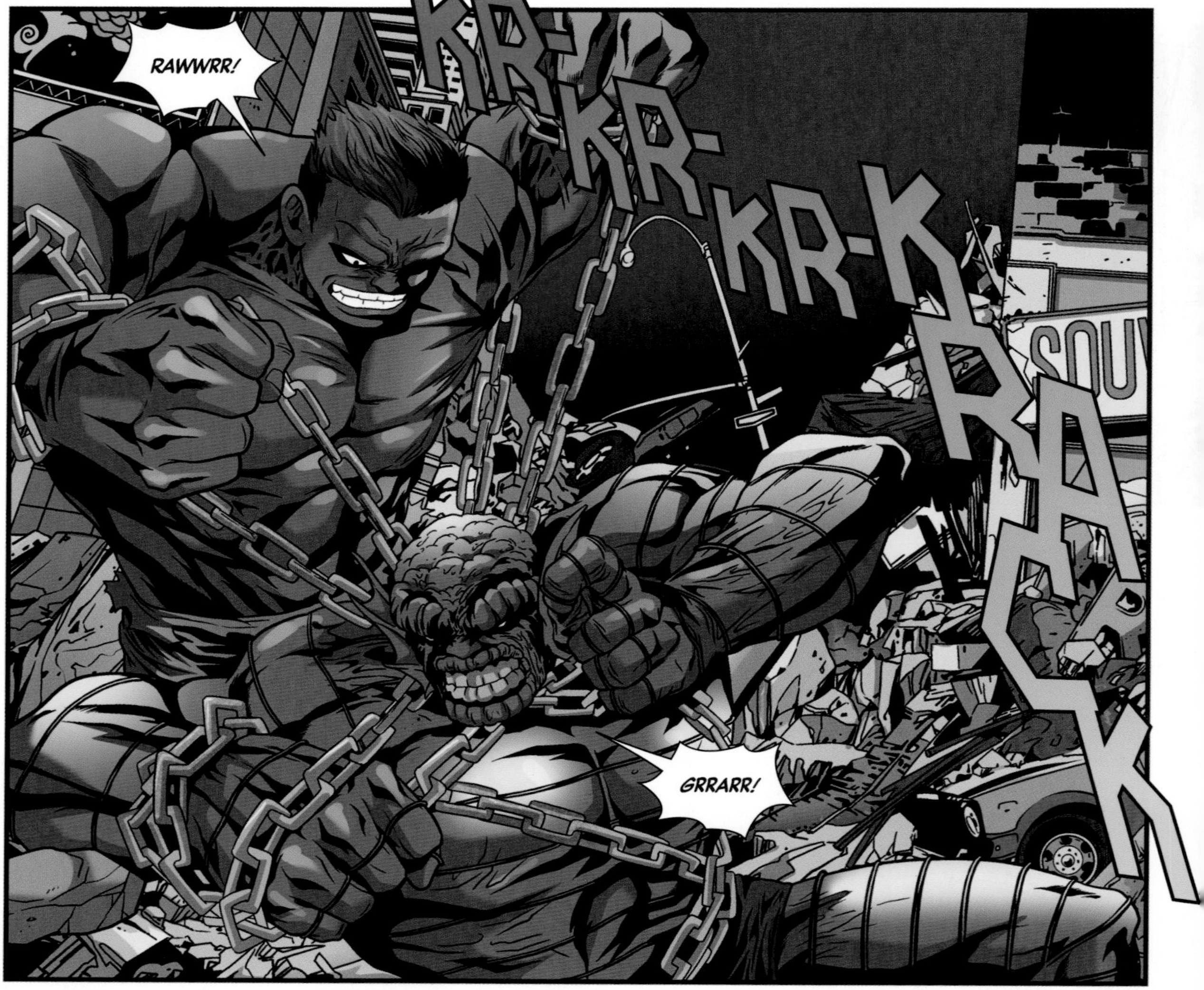
RAWWRR!
KR-KR-KR-KR-KRRACK
GRRARR!

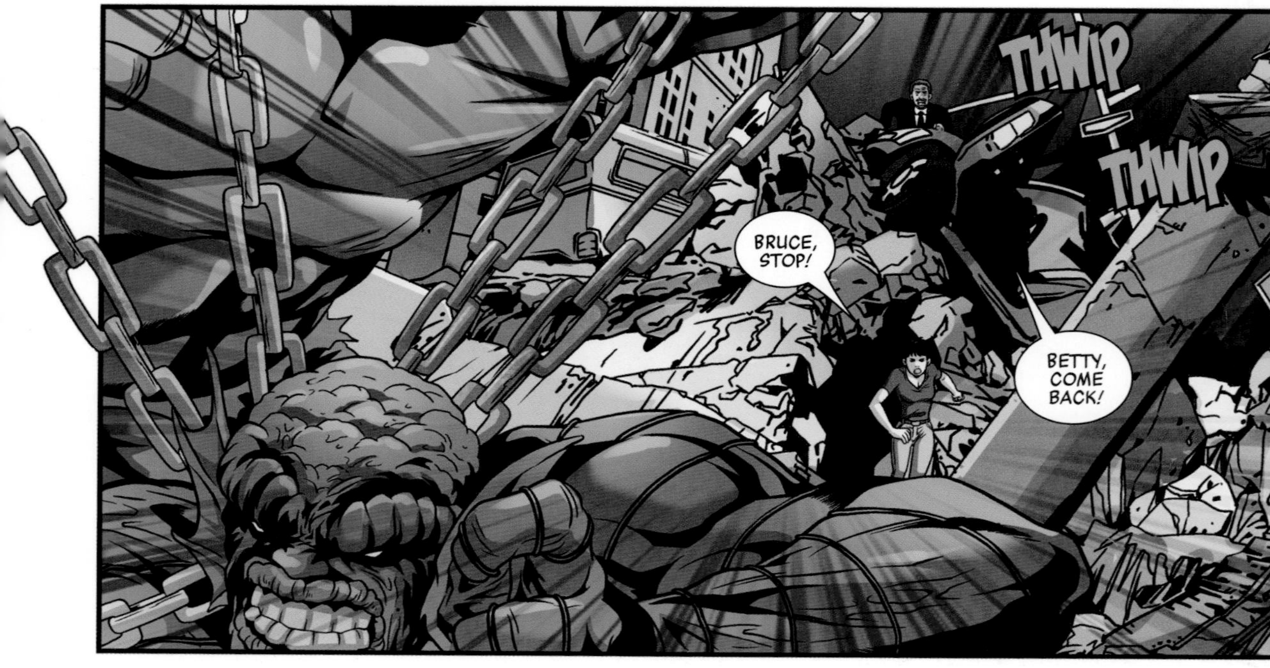
THWIP
THWIP
BRUCE, STOP!
BETTY, COME BACK!

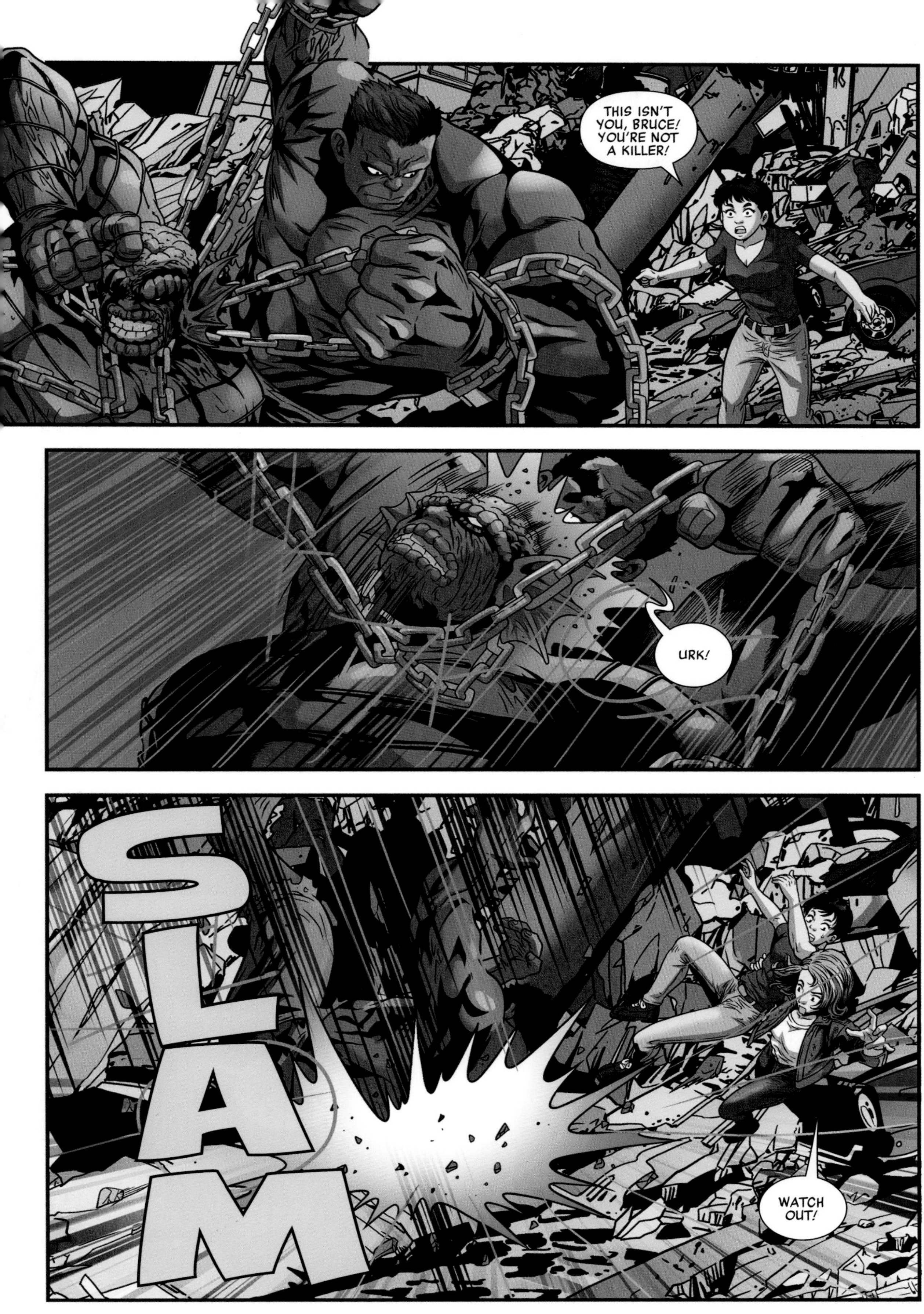
THIS ISN'T YOU, BRUCE! YOU'RE NOT A KILLER!
URK!
SLAM
WATCH OUT!

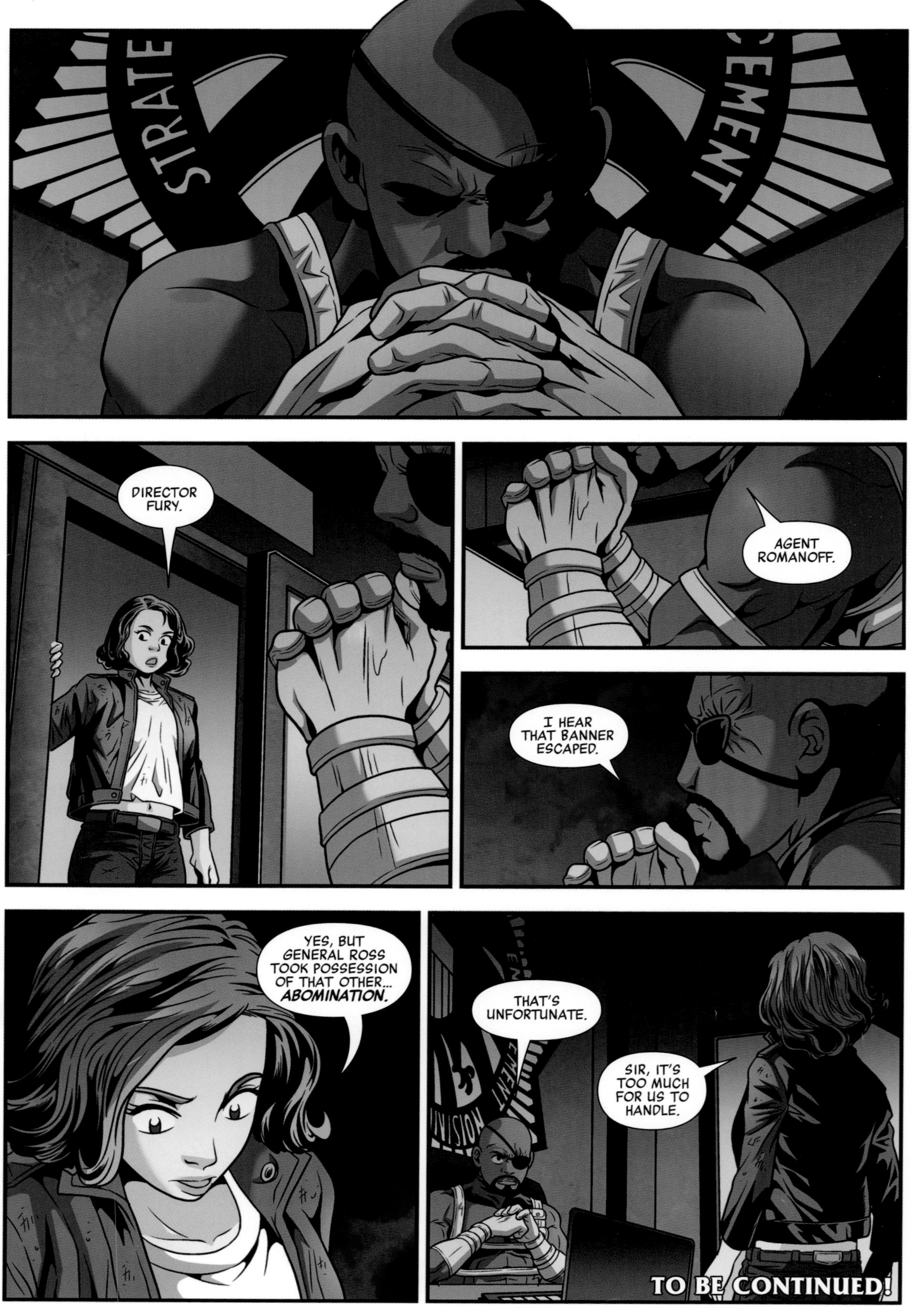
STRATE
CEMENT
DIRECTOR FURY.
AGENT ROMANOFF.
I HEAR THAT BANNER ESCAPED.
YES, BUT GENERAL ROSS TOOK POSSESSION OF THAT OTHER... ***ABOMINATION.***
THAT'S UNFORTUNATE.
SIR, IT'S TOO MUCH FOR US TO HANDLE.
TO BE CONTINUED!